Bedtime Without ARTHUR

Jessica Meserve

ANDERSEN PRESS

Bella has a bear.
A very special bear called Arthur.

He is as **brave** as a knight.
He is as **strong** as ten elephants.

And he does karate.

When Bella sleeps,

Arthur is BUSY.

He guards the bed and keeps away monsters that come sneaking from the shadows.

Safe in her bed,
Bella dreams
of her favourite things,
like rainbows
and rainforests.

One morning, Arthur was worn out from so much karate.

Bella made him his favourite breakfast of toast and honey, and then tucked him up snug in bed.

That evening, when the moon had risen full and white, Bella went to her room to give Arthur a slice of pizza for supper.

Bella pulled back the quilt and...

...yowled,

"Arthur!"

He was gone.

Bella **searched**

and **searched**.

Bella's mum looked upstairs.
Bella's dad looked downstairs.
Bella's brother, Finley,
looked worried.

None of them could find Arthur
ANYWHERE.

Mum said, "We'll find him tomorrow."

Dad said, "He'll turn up."

Finley said, "Sorry."

But Bella didn't believe them.
Her lip trembled as she
climbed into bed.

Bella couldn't sleep.
She was sure there were
MONSTERS
watching and waiting.

Bella squeezed her eyes tight shut.
She fell asleep dreaming of

FIRE-BREATHING DRAGONS,
SLUGS
and grizzly bears.

In the morning, Bella was exhausted.

She couldn't juggle.

Even the ice cream didn't cheer her up.

And at bedtime there
was still
no sign
of Arthur.

The wind began to

blow and howl.

Bella woke with a start.

She saw things looming and scratching at the glass.

Bella leapt out of bed and ran as fast as she could across the hallway into her brother's room.

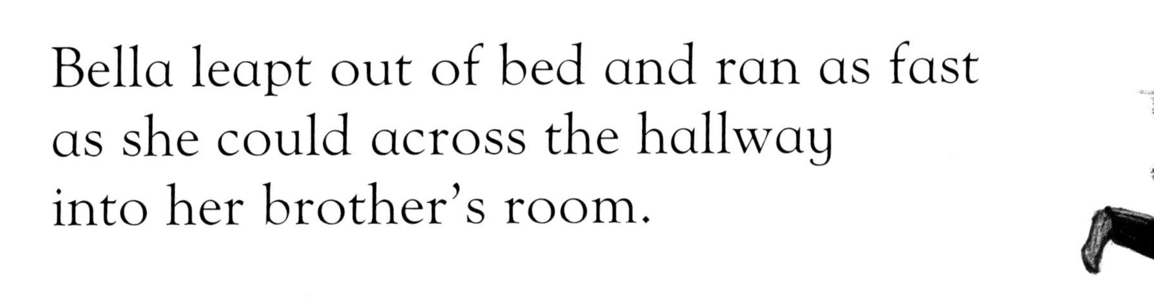

Finley was sound asleep. Bella began climbing into his cot.

Peeking from under the blanket, she saw the tip of a soft, furry nose.

It was Arthur!

Bella was **so** happy to see him . . .

. . . but she was
very angry with her
brother for taking him.

She grabbed Arthur and started back to her room.

Left all alone, Finley was afraid.
"Monsters!" he cried.
Bella pretended not to listen.

"Serves him right," she thought
as she reached the door.

Bella looked back at her brother.
She saw Finley's eyes, wide and full of tears,
and her anger melted away.

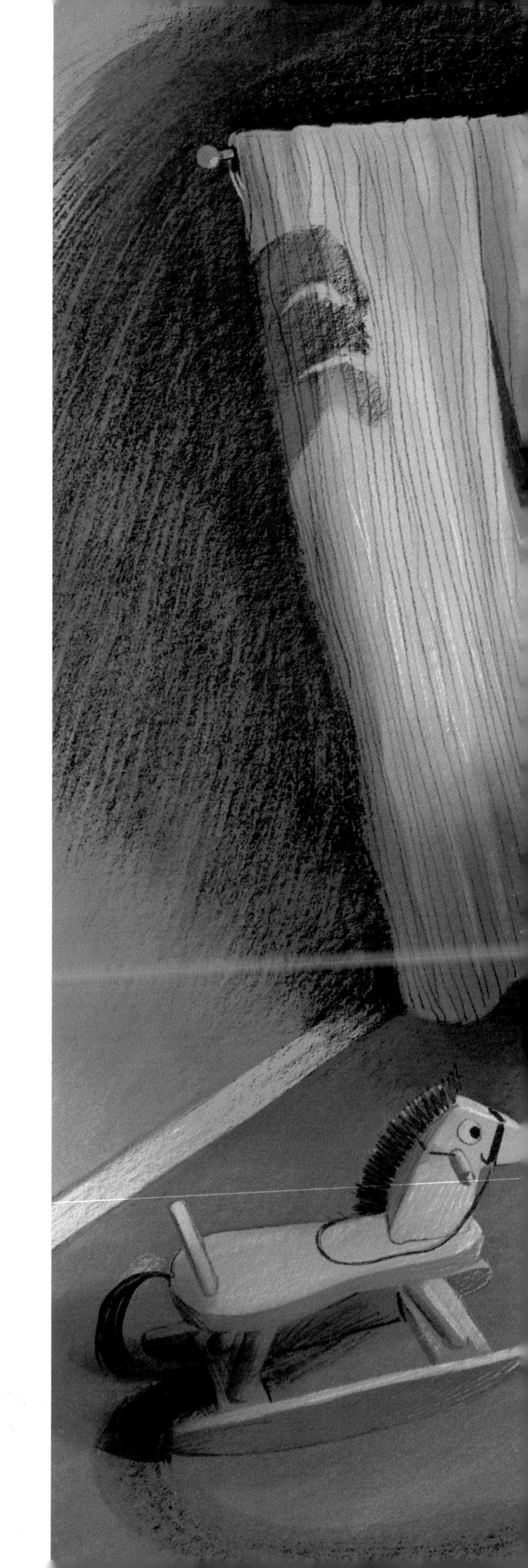

Bella realised that Finley needed Arthur more than she did. Finley wasn't nearly as strong and brave as she was.

Bella took Arthur back to Finley and tucked them both up in bed. "Don't be scared, Finley, Arthur will look after you."

Bella felt braver and
braver with each
step she took back
to her room.

When at last she climbed into bed, Bella felt as brave as a knight. All the monsters shook with fear and fizzled into nothing.

That night Bella slept long and deep and dreamt of all her favourite things.

And so did Finley.